Advance Praise for *Bitter Water Opera*

"I found *Bitter Water Opera* mesmerizing. It reminded me of a book I loved when I was young, written by Alain-Fournier, called *The Wanderer*. A book dense and delicious with God-made language and violent emotion. This is an original for the twenty-first century."

—Fanny Howe, author of *Love and I*

"A lush and dreamy 'storybook-like' novel, reminiscent of Leonora Carrington and Sylvia Townsend Warner, *Bitter Water Opera* asks if we can change our lives—or make choices at all—if we can dwell in possibility 'as if permanently,' if we can allow enchantment into 'the realm of the real.' This is a work of subtle, spiritual intelligence."

—Elisa Gabbert, author of *The Unreality of Memory*

"Nicolette Polek's *Bitter Water Opera* is my favorite type of book, a book that *only* its author could write. In these short, propulsive chapters, Polek writes about the biggest questions and creates a new allegory concerning faith and identity. It's a real garden of a book, full of mysteries and mustard seeds. She shows us a door and asks us to open it, to see what others cannot see. I was astonished."

—Scott McClanahan, author of *The Sarah Book*

"Read *Bitter Water Opera* for the beautiful theologically brilliant prose and also for Gia, its heroine, whose wonder and longing pull a mentor-spirit out of the netherworld. 'The world seemed more broken than usual,' writes Nicolette Polek, a feeling, in our current moment, impossible not to identify with. But the grace and limerence in these pages helped me and I believe they will help you."
—Darcey Steinke, author of *Flash Count Diary*

"Exuberant and improbable, *Bitter Water Opera* is a wonder work of noticing. At times a field guide, a compass, a low-key pilgrimage. Built with each precise line, a chimera of meaning comes into startling focus by its end. The effect of the haunted observer at the center of this limerent, faith-shaped novel is measureless. I wanted to travel with her indefinitely."
—Marie-Helene Bertino, author of *Beautyland*

Bitter Water Opera

Also by Nicolette Polek

Imaginary Museums

Bitter Water Opera

A NOVEL

Nicolette Polek

Graywolf Press

This publication is made possible, in part, by the voters of Minnesota through a Minnesota State Arts Board Operating Support grant, thanks to a legislative appropriation from the arts and cultural heritage fund. Significant support has also been provided by other generous contributions from foundations, corporations, and individuals. To these organizations and individuals we offer our heartfelt thanks.

Published by Graywolf Press
212 Third Avenue North, Suite 485
Minneapolis, Minnesota 55401

www.graywolfpress.org

Published in the United States of America

ISBN 978-1-64445-283-7   (paperback)
ISBN 978-1-64445-284-4   (ebook)

2 4 6 8 9 7 5 3 1
First Graywolf Printing, 2024

Library of Congress Control Number: 2023940114

Cover design: Jeenee Lee

Cover art: Cynthia Talmadge

Blessed are the poor in spirit.
—Matthew 5:3

1

It wasn't impossible; it was simple. I took the letter and put it in my mailbox. I wrote her name in big block letters: MARTA BECKET. She didn't have an address anymore, so I decorated the front of the envelope with watercolors. I included a photograph of myself from childhood, dancing as a toad in my elementary school's production of *The Wind in the Willows*, and a pressed Whirligig daisy. At the time it was something like a prayer.

The next week she showed up. I was rearranging the living room furniture when I noticed a figure through the blinds. I opened the door. She had a small bag that contained my letter, a pair of lime-green shoes, and long cigarettes. I know this because I later went through her things while she was sleeping.

"Marta," I said, and she immediately asked to rest, so I showed her to the back room where I kept my gardening shears and an air mattress for guests.

That evening I was a wreck. *What would Marta eat?* I despaired, and drove through the fog to the market at the edge of the woods. Inside, ABBA songs played over speakers as a stock boy in dress slacks watched me search for special things.

I purchased $250 worth of groceries: duck eggs, pickled cactus, black garlic, and other impractical, elysian foods. I bought plumeria lotion and slippers with stitched dragons on them. The groceries made the car smell like custard, and the sky turned a dark purple as I gripped the wheel.

Marta slept all through the night, even when lightning

struck the neighbor's tree and sent it through the roof of the shed. In the morning, I found her slowly moving through the backyard like a heron, collecting branches from the storm. She was wearing shiny blue underwear, and looked much younger than I, even though she died when she was ninety-two years old.

Dear Marta,

I found your pictures by chance in a library archive. In one, you're a girl in a gown. Your hand touches a bird-cage. In another, you're older. Standing in a simple dress. A cactus and your Amargosa Opera House behind you. You lived in the desert alone, surrounded by the things of your making. You, the once great ghost-town dancer, painter, actress, writer, musician, performer, one-woman show. I danced ballet until my father forbade it. I painted and took acting classes. When you were my age, you left Manhattan to dance your own dances.

At night, I drive on the highway. I pull toward exits that go somewhere far. I switch lanes, but never end up leaving. I cannot bring myself to leave the things that make me small.

I read your memoir, watched your documentary. Like a time line, I formed a life's shape. I wonder if you, too, are able to see my life in full, and could be brought down to attend to it. I dreamt that we walked through the desert. We shared an apple.

Yours, Gia

When I first found Marta's picture she reminded me of my mother. Slim with black hair. My mother didn't have an opera house in the desert, but she had her small bedroom at the front of the house with:

> two windows
> plastic solar-powered flowers that "danced" on
>   the windowsill
> an Audubon clock that played different bird calls
>   on the hour
> shelves filled with books on gardening and how
>   to teach yourself Hebrew
> a yarn collection, organized by material
> the book of Proverbs opened on the table.

Similarly alone, my grandmother insisted that she was a burden to others. She banished herself to an apartment with the Catholic TV channel and potato salad. Of my aunts: one was a nun; another cured her depression by swimming with horses and disappearing into the sea. What would become of me, if not follow suit? So I fled them. Marta was different. She built an accessible grand gesture. When she disappeared, she didn't *disappear*. Like a curtain, concealing and revealing, the opera house tethered her to the public.

Marta and her husband, Tom, were vacationing in Nevada, as the story goes. One morning they awoke in a windstorm to a flat tire on their trailer. On foot, Marta found an empty white adobe complex with an abandoned hotel, offices, a café, and, lastly, through a courtyard of tamarisk trees and a door, she saw a theater, with kangaroo rats and a water-warped stage.

"As I peered through the tiny hole," she said, "I had the distinct feeling that I was looking at the other half of my life. The building seemed to be saying, 'Take me. Do something with me. I offer you life.'"

Marta and Tom moved into their trailer while they renovated. The desert was occupied by alfalfa and ostrich farms, wild horses, mesquite beans, and wind. Marta hated the wind for how it made emptiness emptier. They purchased lawn chairs and corduroy curtains, turned coffee cans into theater lights. Marta's aloneness became something more permanent. She saw herself mirrored in the discarded buildings and the stray cats in town. She rehearsed all day and sometimes taught ballet to the local children, who would later come to her opening performances dressed in pajamas.

Tom changed too, from a big-city businessman into a desert bartender; a man in a cowboy hat who wasn't set up to live in the dust.

A day passed and Marta and I hadn't spoken yet. Felt fretful. Desired having long conversations in a hushed tone on the phone with someone who would share my awe or advise me on the situation.

I had a missed call from my mother.

I pushed the phone under a couch cushion.

Things in the house were missing, taken by Peter when he boxed them. I had stormy landscape paintings but no coffee table. An ornate lamp and an air mattress but no dog or cutting board. I was on leave from the film department at Shepherd College, and surrounded by half-finished projects that fell apart when Peter left. I had small savings and no social media accounts, which I deleted to watch movies on my laptop in the dark. I had an Ambien prescription to fill and a sour spot searching my stomach. I was stuck at the start of something.

I looked out the window. No Marta. Bits of paper littered the grass. My soft-spoken yet rapacious gossip of a neighbor had begun placing flyers in my mailbox for events at her church. I put them in the recycling when she wasn't looking. Occasionally the wind knocked over the bins and the invitations ended up strewn about. Inevitable. Was this doom? I sat on the pink tile of the bathroom. I only remembered each day as it occurred.

Marta remembered all the way back to the moment before she was born. She had once told this to a television reporter, who seemed disturbed and sweaty. But Marta insisted. She remembered looking through an open window at a long white room. She saw her mother in a hospital bed murmuring to her belly. Marta stressed that she could see her own future . . . special-hearted, surrounded by sand, the letter A . . . she could sense it strongly, then a gust of wind came up from behind her and brought her into the hospital room.

This was the kind of woman I thought I would be. Alone and powerful with creation. In childhood, I refused to go to church for months because I disliked that women were made second, like an afterthought, in Genesis. When I told my mother, she laughed and quoted one of her favorite theologians that there is also "an ascending line in creation: from inanimate matter, to plants, lower animals, mammals, man, and finally, women."

Many of our conversations were like this, gridlocked at paradoxes—how greatness is in weakness and the last are first, how in little there is enough, and how all these contradictions were contained in the life of someone who descended into and out of death in order to raise us all. It didn't matter if she was or wasn't right. A veil covered my heart, which opened to another veil, and another veil.

Marta was born in 1924, the same year that Death Valley Junction was built, the place that would later become her Amargosa Opera House. Some things are set from the very start.

Later, Marta wanted to be buried alongside her horses.

I'm not certain if that ended up happening, and I couldn't imagine a polite way to ask.

Marta got through without needing, grieving, or waiting on someone, and now, after death, I was her witness, hoping that she, in some act of imitation on my part, could fix my life.

Marta made me spaghetti for lunch. I curtsied before she sat down. She didn't notice. I was mortified. The table was dressed in a purple cloth and there were wax animal candles—a tiger, an elephant, a goose—that I used for special occasions.

"Marta," I said.

She peered at me.

She ate in a focused way. I put Strauss on in the background, a composer whom I had read Marta enjoyed. By the way she placed her fork down and listened, I gathered that the "Emperor Waltz" made her remember something. All it made me remember was an awkward babysitter I once had, who insisted I waltz with her at the playground.

I was too nervous for noodles, so Marta offered me strawberries for dessert. She put her hand on mine as she ate them.

"Marta," I blurted again. I felt like an octopus in a matchbox. Fanaticism, I'd been told, can be a form of repressed doubt, as irony is a form of concealed enthusiasm. She smiled this time.

She got up and closed the curtains. She lifted her arms and moved around the kitchen like falling ash. She hummed a meandrous melody and cleaned the surfaces while I washed dishes. Together we blew out the candles. I walked through the living room with a lightning bolt in my heart.

Marta noticed everything. The way I lingered at the front steps sifting through the mail; how I wore my bathrobe throughout the day; how I left my thermos in the car; or how the neighbor sat on the front steps knitting, and would pause around five in the evening to stare down the street as though expecting someone. Whoever it was never came.

After dinner Marta sketched parts of the day, then tacked the sketches on the walls of the back room. Her watercolors hung on the clothing line that ran between two young oaks. Ribbons were tied to the tips of branches. On sunny days, she sat in the yard on a chair and closed her eyes. I'd find her with a sketch of a dragonfly resting on her knee. She saw everything in terms of ballet. Horses pirouetted; branches arabesqued.

I loved Les Blank; Peter loved Errol Morris. I shot the footage and Peter edited. Our last project was about the men who rescued hundreds of pigs from the rubble of an earthquake in Japan. Another was about sisters who made plum preserves for an entire town after a string of mysterious deaths. I once believed that the highest aspiration was to be someone who had *an eye for things*, but over time I'd lost the sense of *why* and *what for*, and thus forgot to pay attention, pick things up and feel their shapes, revere and share them, and so they'd fade.

I walked through the back room when Marta was elsewhere, and sifted through her sketches. In my bedroom I saw an orange button. I picked it up and put it in an old mint tin to remember something.

There are other remote theaters in the world: Dalhalla in Sweden, which is 168 feet down the center of a limestone quarry, surrounded by water and chipped cliffs; Red Rocks Amphitheatre in Colorado, the nexus between the Great Plains and the Rocky Mountains; and the legendary Amazonas Theater in Brazil, featured in Werner Herzog's *Fitzcarraldo*, about a man who dreams of building an opera house in the jungle. Places people could barely reach. No audience, critics, needs or desires for art.

For Marta, this wasn't for the novelty money-making attraction, or the niche music festivals. She stayed there in a kind of solitude. No bustling production crews, glitterati and flutes of champagne on opening nights. Only sand and dry summers. She filled the theater with her favorite things, often performed alone—strictly her own choreography—and died. It seemed that she willed one thing into being, and promised that after death she would remain there. She didn't just create the opera house, but became it, too.

I had developed a fascination with this particular sort of landmark. I kept a list of places in a blue spiral notebook. On message boards I read about various labors of love and small-town monuments. I fixated on destinations like a lawn ornament in someone's yard "that bleeds, then weeps, then smiles, according to its owners"; a hot spring caused by underground pressure, "conveniently located behind a bar," that drunk patrons drop eggs into and pull out hard-boiled; a palace of pebbles constructed by a French mailman; an underground citrus orchard; "the loneliest museum that commemorates a town decreasing rapidly"; the tallest Lady of Guadalupe in the world, in a field in Ohio; or the Palace of Depression, a house made of junk built by a former gold miner in an attempt to prove that anything is beatable and that "the only real depression is a depression of individual ingenuity."

I told Peter a guest was staying over, so he picked me up. I moved notebooks and recording equipment off the passenger seat. Driving around, we tried to find a good place to stop.

"Somewhere that won't be ruined by a sour conversation," I said, pressing my knees to the door, but instead voiced something that sounded like "Mmrnmh."

"Here?" He gestured toward the parking lot at a trailhead.

I told him nowhere near the woods. As we continued, the list got longer. I didn't want to talk about messy loose ends near the library where I would write, the park square with white benches, the observatory or the conservatory of flowers, the road that led to the giant DNA sculpture at the top of the hill. I remembered that a roommate in college had warned me about something called Stone Tape Theory: how strong negative emotions get soaked up by the materials nearby—stones, chairs, trees—and then get released later and played back like recordings, or ghosts.

"It's a loop," she had said, face down on my bed. "The broken world points its finger at its brokenness and continues to break." Her mouth was buried into the pillow. She sounded like a frog. I had suspected our entire dorm room was already afflicted.

We turned down an unfamiliar street with oak trees and a lemonade stand. Peter placed the keys on the dashboard, something I had seen my father do when he was pulled over by police. A small gesture to show that he was willing to comply.

"Maybe you should look at what you've done," Peter said, pointing a long finger.

The windows fogged, a child bounded across the street with a basket of lemons, and a light rain came down as I opened the door of the car. I cut through backyards and side streets and watched his car slowly creep down the street and then finally away.

When I approached my porch, I couldn't bring myself to go inside. My pants, wet with rain, stuck to the rocking chair, weighing me down.

I heard a motion behind me. Marta tapped me on the shoulder.

"Come inside and get dressed. I'm taking you to a ballet."

She was holding a towel and some dry socks. Her voice was sparkling, like Marni Nixon or Saint Cecilia, and her face was elegant and equine. Something about her reminded me of a movie . . . where the angel watches over the sad trapeze artist . . . I couldn't think of the name. I followed Marta inside.

Marta's first tragedy was *Swan Lake*. Her father often had extra tickets for reviewing theater events, but this time he gave them to her. She was terrified. Crowds pushed. The theater was an enormous bronze cave . . . she sat between two women who gasped when the curtains went up.

"The dancers move as if tidal waves and other disasters were inside them," Marta said, leaning over the armrest in the theater. "Not only was Odette cursed to the body of a swan by day, she had to live in a lake made entirely from her mother's tears . . . I die a dozen times, especially when the prince marries the wrong girl."

When Marta was a child, her mother brought home handkerchiefs and Marta choreographed dances for them. Marta moved them like swimmers while her mother disappeared behind doors. Her mother was melancholic and her father lived elsewhere. Their house was made from dark wood, stained glass, and French doors. Outside were woods, and in the woods there was no sorrow, only dew, stars, and bugs. Marta loved the smell of crushed ferns, moss, cold salamanders and their slime. She loved fog-horns and being left alone. She hated Wagner's *Ring* cycle, overeducated people, her doctor and her gray cape, and practicing piano scales.

When I was twelve I waited for my loneliness to be broken by a noodly neighbor boy with long blond hair. I had a poster of Baryshnikov in my room and listened to Tchaikovsky in the bath. I lived in a small, cluttered house, soiled with dirt, but imagined that it glowed in veneer and satin. I wondered what it would have been like if Marta and I were in the same audience when we were both twelve. Crossing eyes at each other in the dark, desiring tragedy and grace.

We were children who played the imagination game. I could sit behind a dirty piece of driftwood on the lakeshore and imagine figures emerging from the sand. Even in unseeable places, even at the bottom of the ocean, there were large, soaring things, with beautiful tunes I'd never heard before.

Marta insisted on sitting in the back seat. I had never pictured her in the context of a car before. It would have been more natural if she levitated alongside me, like a sidecar. I snuck glances at her in the rearview mirror.

The window was down and she stuck her nose out into the wind.

We drove from the ballet in silence.

I slowed the car at a yellow light. A shake of dread passed over me. Oh, but Marta, there were secrets. Hidden things behind doors, drawers, faces I believed I understood and faces I later didn't. Resentment, too. I'd shout Peter out of a restaurant, then sweep it under the mat. Eventually many things accumulated. My foot caught on the corner and everything scattered. Marta, have you ever broken a mercury thermometer? Have you ever pretended to be blind to your own lies?

Marta leaned forward in her seat and offered me a long cigarette. She put it in my mouth, lit it. The smoke tasted soft, like walnut shavings, or an unsugared meringue.

When we got home Marta excused herself to bed. I waited until I heard soft sleep sounds through the door, then slipped on Marta's lime-green shoes and stepped outside.

Lights lined the sidewalks and I walked down the center of the empty street, softly humming a tune from *Swan Lake*. At night the road was long like a desert road, with no end or beginning. At the top, a late-night train glowed over the hill.

I tried to remember how the imagination game worked . . . all I could imagine were theater set versions of places and things. Instead of a nighttime forest, I pictured myself walking through plywood cuts of moonlit bushes, silver painted rocks, sunset curtains. I continued guiding myself through fake living rooms with doors that couldn't open and birds that sang on loop through speakers. I stepped stage to stage, but when I looked out, a calcified version of myself stared back from the audience, asking me to consider what I'd done.

After lunch in the summers, I used to walk a two-mile loop at Walby Point, while Peter went back to the studio.

One afternoon, midway on the trail, I saw a colleague whom I'd often pass on campus. He was older and distracted, and wore a green baseball hat. From afar, we nodded hello as we often nodded hello in the halls, and as we approached each other, he noted how pleasant the air was, then asked if he could join me on my walk.

We continued for longer than my usual route, taking the overlook trail, finding surprising synchronicities between us: our fathers were both furniture makers; we attended the same absurd Canadian polka camp as teens. The walk felt simple; we were unrushed to return to our respective lives, and delighted by the unlikely connection. We pointed out things we noticed along the path—a fallen tree that made the letter B, an abandoned sock, something warbling in a tree.

There was a row of crab apple trees at the top of the trail, sturdy and mangled with age, and I climbed onto one of the lower branches to look out at the vista. He turned toward me to say something, and as he did, I caught his hand. I didn't understand why. A thrilled impulse. He moved closer, as though this was intended all along. In an instant, the levity from our walk extinguished under irreversible fog. We stayed there pressing each other against the crab apple tree, until the bark dug into my back and the sun fell from dark orange to gray.

I didn't see him again, and crafted a series of lies to

cover up the evening. I'd opened a door onto something that had no continuity with my life. I never spoke of it to Peter. A maddening anguish evolved. The event ambiently touched everyone around me. My mother sent me Psalms; I never read them. Peter bought me glass bookends; I shattered them.

I knew people had this sort of encounter all the time, and yet it was my own capacity for dishonesty that disturbed me, along with my spiraling need to hide it.

At the time, the only plausible-seeming exit from trouble was to enter it further, so I stopped walking the two-mile loop altogether and found odd, discrete entanglements with acquaintances and on dating apps, passed my phone number to attractive cashiers, and took a trip to visit an old pen pal, who then undressed me in his large, spotless kitchen with an extensive display of fish knives. My relationship with Peter collapsed, and I was left with Marta, to whom I couldn't confess either.

The world seemed more broken than usual. When I'd asked for a leave from the college, I'd gone into my supervisor's office and sat in her Alessandro Mendini chair. She leaned across her desk and said that "everyone is filled with heaviness these days." The air conditioner blasted as she poured herself an amaretto. She'd been thinking a lot about emotions: rage, lust, panic, grief. "What about hope?" I asked. She paused, as if not having heard me, then invited me to a panel discussion as she signed my paperwork. She returned to her Mac desktop. As I went to leave, I heard a muffled shout, something like "Errogggo." My boss pointed at her belly and apologized. She was so hungry.

Before Marta arrived, I had been sleeping upwards of fifteen hours most nights, slipping away in front of screens and flipping dissociatively through books during research sessions at the library. Days trying to dissolve into rooms, and then into a small pit at the center of my head.

Whenever guilt set in, Marta appeared, carrying a dishrag, or a box of colored pencils, or a pomegranate to deseed. One morning I cried instead of eating breakfast, so she brought me a shiny beetle from the yard. It was purple and Marta touched her finger to my lips so I would listen. The beetle made thin, metallic sounds. It sounded like it was singing "Ave Maria."

I showed Marta the charcoal drawings inside the garage. They had been there since Peter and I moved in. They were figurative, and terrifying. When Peter cut the lawn, I would wander into the garage and scheme a transformation for them. The drawings, each time, unsettled me, and I would leave quickly. There were three main illustrations:

> Crucified figure, levitating over a roof. Crossed-
> out eyes.
> Large woman with a square womb. Little girl
> inside. Noose to the side.
> Back of a naked figure facing a crudely drawn
> floor plan of the house.

I had always attributed any unknown unrest in our home to these drawings. I even considered that they were responsible for the thrilled impulse that seized me at the overlook. Sometimes scampering sounds descended from our attic at night, like trapped charcoal spirits transmitted from the garage.

Marta paced around the garage with her hands behind her back. By the end of the day the garage was wet white.

There had been a flood a few years after Marta moved into Death Valley Junction. Rain from the Funeral Mountains came down into the valley and filled the opera house with over a foot of mud. With every step Marta took, her shoes filled with sludge, so she took them off and waded barefoot through the damage. So much of her past— photographs, sketches, letters, costumes—had been destroyed by a mountain named after a ceremony of death.

Once the wet clay had been squeegeed, Marta started on a mural that expanded through the interior of the opera house. She wanted to keep the past alive by painting an audience of all the people who formed her. She painted images of theater balconies and filled them with mother superior and her sisters, a Gypsy fortune teller, a guest drinking wine out of a high-heeled shoe, members of the Spanish Renaissance, her cats, a bullfighter eating a mango.

"My talents are my friends," she would say insistently to visitors who remarked on her solitude. She wanted a castle. Every woman wants a castle.

Tom had been staying in brothels, she said to me. We were sitting in the backyard eating watermelon, our sticky hands speckled with dried paint.

He resented the way she was free of him, when she danced and painted for hours. He used to be her manager on Broadway, but out in the desert he couldn't manage her. Hippies moved next door, selling sand candles. Tom became their friend. Between them and the women of Ash Meadows Lodge, he became capricious and glum. Marta visited a brothel herself, to learn how to keep him happy. She admired their feathers and face paint but they couldn't help her.

She told me how she worked long, rapt hours, capturing light on the mural. He worked through the night in a bordello in town. He wanted touch while her world became unsexual, abstract, and closer to what she imagined heaven to be like. The more she obsessed over the mural, the unhappier he became. As the women of Ash Meadows had predicted, he left her.

"I was tired of trying to be a good wife. I had been a good daughter for so long then; what I really wanted to be was a good dancer, a fine painter, a good me," she said.

She had known that if she was going to do important work, the unimportant things would have to fall away.

The mural, she told me, took five years. Those were the happiest years of her life. She described a figure that she painted holding a scroll that read in Latin, "The walls of this theater and I dedicate these murals to the past, without which our times would have no beauty." At the time I took it to be true, but now had a creeping sense that beauty came from somewhere else entirely.

Turning back to the empty garage walls, I asked myself aloud what to put on the walls. Marta suggested I lift my heart up.

In order to inspire my mural, Marta took me to the nearby estate of an old landscape painter. We signed up for an hour-long tour.

In the tour group, a young boy with a large nose asked if the bouquet on the table was real. "All these flowers are fake," the guide said, bending down to reach eye level, "to keep out bugs that would eat the paintings." He patted the small blond head and we continued into the next room.

The house was covered with layers of dust, which the original owner instructed never to clean in order to preserve the natural life span of the paint. Only the members of the church could touch the walls. Their fingerprints remained there forever. Marta placed her hand onto the wall when the rest of the tour group moved on to the next room.

The Victorians had a fear of empty spaces, so they'd overdecorate, the tour guide explained, pointing at the corners of the house, filled with chairs, rugs, statuettes, rolled-up maps, end tables, desks, ashtrays, umbrella holders, pottery, paintings everywhere, large wooden egrets, gongs, hourglasses, historical tiles, grandfather clocks, rusty levered boxes, an abacus in front of another abacus, calendars, chimes, opera masks, and the walls themselves were covered in elaborate wallpaper—patterns of overlapping leaves, curly vines, snails, fountains, cherubs, small red birds. Victorians even covered the legs of furniture, afraid of that pulsing unknown.

When we walked out onto the veranda, the tour guide pointed out trees in the distance that the painter had obsessively planted. The field would have otherwise been bare.

I went on an afternoon walk by the rose garden and sat beside a peeling eucalyptus tree. I fidgeted between a radish sandwich, a coffee cup, people-watching, and searching Marta Becket on the internet. This was shortly eclipsed by texting Peter, who lived down the street. He said he'd be "over in a sec" so I sat more at ease, more disappointed, grumbling into my sandwich, making crumbs onto my lap.

Peter regarded me, sat suddenly, and asked how I was.

I didn't know what to say, except to remark on the pine cones in the courtyard. "They swell shut when you put them in water."

He nodded blankly.

I pointed to the bird bath where a pine cone sat at the edge.

"How are you?" I asked, panicked.

"Oh, you know," he said, offering a small smile. Silence made its slow pass.

"Maybe we can see each other again," I offered, body wilting under the anxiety of the encounter.

We agreed on lunch. I could finally tell him, I considered. Though I didn't know what coming clean would solve.

When he left, I put my head in my hands.

I wanted to be a someone for anyone who would think of me with a soft heart. That you'd imagine me in your living room after I left for work. Standing by the piano and the curtain drawn, you'd notice the wisteria on the terrace. I turn to look at you. You see me in slow motion, smiling, turning. You'd remember thinking, I'm in love, I'm in love.

I went to my office at Shepherd College to retrieve some things from my desk. Elaine, my former office mate, left the department right before me, so the office now was unoccupied. I pushed myself into my broken swivel chair and felt tears well up.

We weren't the only ones—there had been a suspiciously low retention among our colleagues. The departments were emptying out, everyone in search of new jobs and towns, treatments and higher salaries. One left to become a personal trainer. We were all being bested by an educational machine that ran on spurious promise, a part of some larger cultural milieu of restlessness and indecision, shame and lack. It was as though everyone was involved in elaborate and top-secret cover-ups of their own selves.

Elaine was always in crisis, which allowed me to abandon my own. We became friends when she had decided to leave her husband by removing one object per day from their apartment. She'd put it in a duffel bag and leave as if she was going to the gym. Instead she'd take a bus to a property by the water. There was an empty white room in the base of an abandoned water tower, which had been untouched by squatters and municipal officials for years. From their apartment she could see the tower, but from the tower all she could see were expanses of blue. She put a padlock on the room's door and began to fill it. "You can't do that," I remembered telling her, shaking my head. "You can't leave something that way," even though I didn't know what the right way would be.

In the mornings the husband attended to himself in the full-length mirror, before heading along to the Air and Space Museum, where he was a security guard. Elaine watched him turn sides in his reflection like a minnow catching light, combing his long black hair and shaving speckles from his jaw. The mirror had a gold frame, ornamented with leaves and trumpets, and had been in her family for years.

She considered telling him her plan to leave. She wanted to tell him how he made her sick, how it drove her mad when there was time left unaccounted for when he was late from work. Was there another woman? She could imagine his response—a sour, vengeful facial expression that would silently curdle the air between them, followed by him leaving for work and ignoring her messages for long enough that she would inevitably frighten herself into thinking that she had made a mistake.

Her method was easy and gradual. With each day she became accustomed to a new life. She'd come into the office and say things like "today was a lamp," or "this weekend was a sugar spoon."

It had taken a year for all of her possessions to get from one place to the other. In that time, she had constructed an entire fantasy of the life that her husband was hiding, involving a busty redhead smothering him on the roof of the Air and Space Museum. Whenever Elaine felt weak-willed or was about to abandon her plan, she imagined her husband gasping and grasping at the woman's folds, or the woman slipping her fingers into his mouth.

She had finally planned to tell him over lunch on a Sunday, but he didn't return from his bike ride until the early evening. Something about telling him at night broke her heart, so they held each other one final time. She pretended to fall asleep. Her husband went to the bathroom to examine his shape. He noticed that the ornamental mirror was gone.

He went into the closets, thinking that the housekeeper had moved it. But instead he found nothingness and walked back into the bedroom in slow shock. Elaine looked at him coolly, instructing him to make a pot of coffee.

It turned out he had no secret life. At least not in the

way she had thought. He was taking care of his brother who had an addiction he was ashamed of, and in the process fell back into his own alcoholism.

This could have been a relief for Elaine, but it was too late. She had already pulled away from him in all the important ways. It wasn't long after that she quit her job.

"Sometimes, you have to bite the bullet at the beginning," a coworker said before she too left the college, "or you end up with a demented life, one molded by the slow glow of cowardice, like a hot molten orb of glass."

I saw Elaine not long after she left, arguing with a Botox-injected blond man over buttered crab. I passed her table and she looked at me as if I was a shadow.

Marta and I sat on a quilt in the backyard with a bottle of tequila and projected *The Red Shoes* onto the side of the shed. We watched Moira Shearer put on her ballet shoes and get taken away, to the shore, the cliff, a large banquet hall, through the circus. I rooted for her to stay with the ballet company and spend her life in love with dancing, while Marta insisted that she should give it up and love a life with the composer. I was surprised.

In the very end, the character got neither.

We lay back and looked up at the sky. Marta told me that the aurora borealis makes a tinny twinkly sound, but few people can hear at that frequency. We were quiet for a few minutes. My eyes fluttered shut. A subphysical tingle spread through my body as I wondered how long I could stay this way, watching characters on screens grow, while I couldn't even bring myself to stand up.

This suspension game was a kind of imagination game.

Like this: I imagined two doors. Through one was a hallway unknowably long and dim, only wide enough for one, which led somewhere imperceivable. Through the other was no hallway, but a room where I've always been. I remained at these two doors and a desire to vanish grew stronger, as if my heart was wrapped in dry gauze, my brain pickled in a griefly vinegar.

This was my condition, simmering in some sort of parenthetical lapse of events in the otherwise planned path. I could escape change for so long that progress was no longer possible. I shut my eyes. My blood pressure felt low, thick like molasses.

I rolled over on the blanket and saw something white nestled in the grass. I squinted. It looked almost like a box, or a kitten. I pulled myself up and approached it curiously, then picked it up.

MEAL KIT PREPARATION VOLUNTEER DAY AND CONTRA DANCE EVENING the church flyer read in blue block letters. I heard a distant singing from my neighbor's porch. I folded the flyer until it became something small enough to fit in my pocket.

Marta stood above me. There she was, standing, speaking.

I clamped the blankets close and tried to turn away, but stopped. The drapes had been drawn. She wore a purple pleated dress and her hair was draped back, as my mother used to wear hers.

Beside me on my pillow was my laptop, and I remembered us coming inside after watching *The Red Shoes* . . . me saying goodnight, and going to my room to try to write an email to Peter explaining what happened at Walby Point and in the year that followed. We planned to get lunch the following day. My stomach sank.

She asked me to get out of bed. She wanted to take me somewhere again, farther than the ballet this time. She was smiling. I told her that I had a date with Peter. I was grumpy and frustrated. Marta was silent, sad. Out of her pocket peeked a map with a pen clipped to it.

Like a big door on a small hinge, she moved uncertainly. If she had ears like a dog they would have been back flat against her head. She shouldn't be here, I thought.

She left the room suddenly. I burrowed under the blankets.

I entered the diner where we agreed to meet. I had phrases written on a piece of paper to keep me focused. Around me couples quietly hunched over Reubens and news-papers. Low ceilings. Frilled red country curtains covered the small windows.

I sat at a corner, arranging the sugar packets to outline the circumference of the table. I tore open a pink packet into the center, then another, and another, until it resembled a soft crystal hill. I blew it and it flattened. I called Peter. His phone was off. I fidgeted with my hands, drawing lines in the sugar piles with my pointer finger.

The couple beside me paid their check and put on their jackets as I glanced at my phone. He wasn't coming. I could feel it.

I remembered a dinner party with Peter when I first moved here to his town. Someone had asked me what led me to move across the country, and my mind drew a blank. Plates of strange foods passed before me as I stammered, trying to form sentences. Saffron and cardamom foam, frozen roses dipped in black salt, liquescent foods encased in glaze, flavored ice disks and rabbit brains in nasturtium leaves. Distracted by lovely noisy things, I tried to recall myself.

The food passed my lips like vapor and left me hungry. I was a stranger there, from a place that had winters, and those new days were marked by the silhouettes of tall palms and the mossy outlines around the bay. We'd take a basketball to the old ruins and pass it between the columns, through clock towers and cemeteries. His hand was large and he'd take mine to tuck into his coat pocket. He'd knock on the window of my office to show me a page in his book. In the morning we'd get muffins and eat them on the stoop beside the bougainvillea trees. I'd stand up to dust the crumbs off my lap, but even the dirt then was clean.

Yet something was always crouching at the door, a large shadowy shape. Was it uncertainty? Where there's wind, a door can slam shut and be kept shut, as well as be blown open, clanging against the side of a newly painted house. Years ago I biked through strong, lifting wind, on the way up to the DNA sculpture with Peter. The road was dark. At the top of the hill, where the giant double helix was, we fell from our bikes in exhaustion and climbed through the metal hydrogen bonds and DNA backbones, our hair flying in every direction. At the end of the horizontal ladder we sat on a bench, where the wind moved us to huddle together, and as I remembered this, a wind was coming through the red country curtains of the diner, blowing things apart.

I looked for Marta, first in her room, then the backyard. In the shed, I looked at our unfinished mural. We had painted a long staircase with people I admired sitting on each step. I had painted a door, a basketball, curtains, a candle, a key.

On the painted steps sat Ingmar Bergman, Krzysztof Kieślowski, Jacques Rivette, Chopin, Ravel, Rachmaninoff, Mother Maria Skobtsova, Barbara Bloom, Remedios Varo, Leonora Carrington, Gogol, Karen Kilimnik, Jane Goodall, Beatrix Potter, Hans Christian Andersen, Remy Charlip, Bruegel, Gertrude Abercrombie, Wong Kar Wai, Tarkovsky, Louis Malle, Dorothea Tanning, many more.

Marta had painted herself at the top of the stairs. She'd finished the shading on the railing and the shadows beneath her figure's feet.

She'd also cleaned the brushes and sealed the paint cans.

Her smock was gone, and so was her red bag in the back room.

Her lime-green shoes were removed from beside her door.

No watercolors hung in the backyard between the trees.

2

I walked down a thin path, spotting in the distance a tall stone wall, as instructed. My wheeled luggage clunked on stones behind me.

The sun was falling and the forest, mostly evergreens, darkened quickly. Farther to my side was a marsh, shaded grayly.

At the stone wall was a sturdy wooden door with large padlocks. Corresponding keys were tied underneath vines to the side of the door.

The owner, Simone, had been pleased to hear from me, urging me to stay for a few weeks in exchange for up-keep. She was a former professor of mine, at the tail end of her overseas sabbatical.

Her house was in the woods outside a small hamlet. I planned to take some time in silence, get myself in order, in a bare environment without distraction. I had long looked to fix my life through other people, so now, I con-sidered, I could try fixing it alone.

In an email describing the property, Simone mentioned a "dramatic heron that visits." She wrote, "Here, when it's dark out, it gets dark dark."

I eagerly pushed my entire weight against the door.

Behind the door was what appeared to have once been tidy but was now overgrown. Split milkweed and cattails suspended over the lawn line. Clusters of cleavers grew around the pond that preceded the main house. I had weeded only once or twice in my life, as a child volunteer at a local botanical garden, but then they were patches so small that the whole of them were in arm's reach.

This space was large, with the pond and a stone path. An empty, greening fountain. The stone wall circled around so high that all I could see from the other side were tree crowns.

I walked through the high grass to a white wooden house, spotted with dirt, with black shutters and a shingled roof.

A lime-green grasshopper sprung off the doorknob.

Everything extremely alive.

Inside was cold and quiet. Downstairs was a living room, a small country kitchen, and a long wooden staircase. Various recesses held tall solitary candles. Rooms furnished with simple wooden furniture, Hammershøi-esque.

I tired quickly, made myself a cup of nettle tea from the cupboard above the kettle, and went upstairs. I got into bed wearing only a T-shirt, under four blankets covered in dust. I set an alarm on my phone. No missed calls or messages. I hadn't told anyone where I had gone. I'd vanished, as I'd always wanted, like Marta Becket and Peter, or Jean Rhys, whose absence went on for twenty years before she released *Wide Sargasso Sea.*

I closed my eyes and lay still, and envisioned everyone I've ever met laughing in a brightly lit house, grazing each other's cheeks with their hands, while I watched from far away in the cold, slowly evaporating into air.

"Some people don't like the quiet," warned Simone in her email. "I had a writer leave early because her dog was sick. She didn't even have a dog."

The space between my heart and lungs sunk and contracted. I took a strawberry-flavored melatonin and found a portable radio in the desk. I brought it under the covers and listened to a droning voice narrate a baseball game.

Falling asleep felt like a warm damp towel sliding down the inside of my head.

Attached to Simone's email was a list of tasks:

> cut, maintain all grass
> clean the fountain
> take away vines
> weedwacker
> paint the shutters black
> pressure wash house

Paragraphs below it described other intricacies of the property: a suggestion to cut my hair and scatter it among plants to deter squirrels and cats; a Xeroxed page from a *Boston Journal of Chemistry* article explaining that "the prevalent tone in nature is the key of E," and that the majority of winged insects harmonize and sound together in "the same symphony"; another article outlining the ancient tradition to orally tell major life events to the bees . . .

I felt tired by the wondrousness of her message. I went back to the task list.

I stood in the center of the property and looked around.

The property felt impossible.

The green ground stretched out before me, none of which I could register.

Through the brambles was a rusted red toolshed where I found a yellow shovel. A tinted window let in enough light to fall onto a pair of gloves. A bug walked across the wall and when I stubbed it with my thumb it left behind a blue smudge. The bug had been alive and then it suddenly wasn't, like a flipped switch. It was that kind of death that I wished for then, like a sniped balloon.

I walked back outside to the center and looked around again. The spot beneath my feet was as good as any to start with, as far as I knew.

I pulled at a few dandelions.

What I was supposed to do would take forever, I thought.

I looked again at the list of tasks. Grass cutting seemed the most familiar, so I went back to the shed and brought out the mower.

I yanked a cord. The machine sputtered then fell silent. I yanked again. Nothing gave.

I pushed the mower across the tall wild grass back to the shed.

Two days passed, then ten.

For breakfast one morning I ate pantry pickles and instant coffee. I stared out the kitchen window upon the exuberant yard. All the wiry greenery, coiling and rising. I noticed specks of dandelions for the first time, fairy-ringing around the fountain. I paused midbite.

A large mass was floating in the center of the pond.

Something that looked like a dead body, on its stomach.

I put down my coffee and rushed outside in bare feet.

From a distance, the body was beige, wearing what appeared to be a camel-colored Burberry trench coat. I stood still, startled and numb, as if I'd touched something at an extreme temperature and it was hard to tell immediately if it was hot or cold.

Was it the dramatic end of some cast-aside lover of Simone's? Or did someone trespass and fall into the pond by accident? The image crossed my mind of a murderer dragging the body through the grass, collecting ticks and mud, with only owls and mice as witnesses. Some kind of warning. The murderer's face gleamed in the moonlight of my saturated worry—it was Peter. Or was the body Peter?

I walked out across the grass until I reached the wooden dock. I flipped over a muddy yellow kayak, and wobbled out into the water. Cold mud coated my toes and miry water splashed into the kayak. My arms were jelly. Once I drew closer to the body, I reached out my paddle and nudged it.

A scream bubbled up so suddenly that the kayak swung from under me. My arms flung and met a net of pond plants. I reached forward, instinctually grabbing onto the soft bloated body, then shrank away, scrambling to the kayak.

A deer, with its eyes eaten away by fish.

Sodden and flashed with adrenaline, I paddled back to shore. Instructions seemed to form naturally in my head as abstract shapes. In the toolshed, I found coils of rope, caked in spiderwebs, and made a wide lasso that would fit around the deer's waist. I paddled back out into the pond and tied one end of the rope to a hook on the kayak, forcing myself to look upon the deer's body. A friend once told me about a near-drowning experience, when the tide pressed her so far down that it felt as though her skin was melting. How did I end up here, and why didn't I have anyone to talk to? I felt singed by panic. I could've had Peter—but I couldn't have, because I desired someone else, and with them I would desire yet another. It was my limerence that I'd masterfully hidden out of my conscience so that it rose out in a moment such as this. It was my limerence for other people that afflicted me, my limerence to be in the future, limerence for the so-called beauty of the past, limerence for other places I had no business living in, limerence for stew when I was eating pie, a limerence so strong that I was always in a world that didn't even exist. My limerent life ran through my head in tandem with my real life, a daydream on steroids, which simultaneously pulsed with dopamine and deflated reality into something transparent and malnourished. My limerent life was a scam, a subterfuge, a patch of quicksand, a treadmill and a trap, a growing of a second person inside myself until I never said what I meant nor knew what I wanted. The deer dragging against the pond made waves as though it was swimming. Who had I become, if not a bag of words? When I was four I filled a getaway bag with two dollars and a book on American quilts. I took the elevator to the tenth floor of our apartment building. Freedom felt like peering out a hallway window for an hour, looking at everyone continue on below. It was my limerence that slowly turned me into the woman I didn't wish to become, like my mother and grandmother, who barricaded themselves away, so that I was shaking alone in the middle of a pond, carrying a noose-like rope, and at the end of it a dead deer, at an empty property protected by a high wall. Everything that I turned to wasn't right. It dragged on limply like a slug, drawing attention to its insufficiency. It wasn't an absence of something—surely not an absence of belief—but a presence of something else, something stubborn that wished to twist with a will of its very own.

For a moment, I glimpsed Marta, pulling the deer across the water with me.

Lugging the deer from the pond to leave on land, I felt a shift, as if something in me had separated or fallen away.

The smell of the deer, searing, like blood and damp garbage, stuck onto me when I was back in the house. I sat in the kitchen, picturing it falling through a layer of ice in winter. I imagined it remaining there, drifting in a cold world until the thaw.

After some time passed I stood up. I went to make canned beans for lunch, wondering how much time it would take for the vultures to come and nibble the body clean.

At first the smell continued. It wormed around the property like a slatch, sinewing through the windows. It seemed stuck inside my nose itself, so I swabbed it with a Q-tip soaked in tea tree oil. When the stinging stopped, the smell came back in small shocks like a memory in the periphery. But then the smell faded for good, and with it my revelation. Whatever had surged within me on the pond was gone. Like playing hide-and-seek with a child, something had peeked from behind a tree—a hand or a long tail—long enough for me to spot it, before tucking itself away again.

The next days were gruesomely lost. I seldom left the bed and when I did it was out of necessity. I gorged myself on potatoes and cheese. I wore many sweaters, layers of wool and alpaca to constrict me. The garden continued growing, the fountain continued greening, and the list of caretaking tasks expanded in their urgency so that a chasm grew between them and the possibility of me completing them. I couldn't do it on my own. I didn't even cry, just stared from beneath the blanket like a dead person held down by the weight of dark matter.

Dear Marta, what is this curse? I could hear my department chair listing off reasons I felt the way I did—a combination of things I had no hand in, inherited from the world of childhood and men, people I've never met, things I didn't know were being carved into me through generations, the burden of being this, that, and some other thing. Is this why the desert compelled you? A place where you were responsible only for the things you did, not who you were? Thinking of Marta seemed juvenile, like feeding coins into a hollow aluminum dispenser.

I curled up so completely that I felt that I could look myself in the eyes.

A classmate in college once told me that she discovered, through intensive research, that a great-great-grandmother had endured a shipwreck, something that subsequently altered her so thoroughly that her daughters and granddaughters could feel it in the ways they hurt and moved up the steps of the family home. The classmate brought it up often—"as a descendant of a shipwreck." Everything from flaking on plans to failing her exams somehow traced back to that unfortunate accident, so much so that it replaced her. One year, an international student returned from summer break having survived a terrible boating accident that paralyzed the right side of her body and killed her sister. Within weeks of her return to campus, the shipwreck descendant slapped her in a post office parking lot. Something about stamps, she justified.

The thought terrified me. Pointing at everyone and everything. A victim of myself.

But the smell was gone. At least there was that.

I tried calling Peter, but my phone service couldn't catch. I went to the computer to email him, but the internet was down. I looked toward the bedroom window and saw heavy rain clouds above, then collapsed back into the bed.

Once we wandered into an inverted tower. There was a spiral staircase that descended into the ground like a large well. Smelled like moss and cold stone. A brilliant red bird startled us as it flew up from the bottom and out into the sky. We were the only ones in the tower and when we reached the bottom we found a small tenebrous hallway, a tunnel, that led to more darkness and dripping sounds. In front of the passageway was a DO NOT ENTER sign.

Peter stepped past it while I stayed, afraid to cross the line.

After he had been gone for a short moment, I called his name, thinking how thin and infirm my voice sounded. I thought of Mendelssohn, how when he was twenty years old he visited Fingal's Cave and sat silently inside darkness for an hour before composing and sending to his sister Fanny a beginning draft of *The Hebrides*, which to him evoked the feelings of the cave, the stalactites, the expansive network of emptiness and enclosure, though, according to Mendelssohn, there was not enough "oil and seagulls and dead fish" in the music.

Peter had popped out with a look of glee.

I found myself now in that secret place, but while I called and called out, I burrowed deeper into the tunnel between towers.

The more I stayed in bed, the more I couldn't bear to look at the property. I worried that I wouldn't be able to finish the caretaker tasks in time, that Simone would come home early to find her cottage in deep disorder.

I walked downstairs . . . the bare wood . . . the Shaker furniture . . . stark and vile. All the beige curtains drawn . . . pale like maggots . . . quiet rooms . . . lone lamps lit to reveal nothing beneath them. I wanted to cover up the white walls with slogans and advertising . . . cover the windows with wooden slabs so that the house became forgettable . . . I stood in the living room shivering.

I didn't know for certain if it was day or nighttime until I pulled myself outside into the dark yard. The grass had taken on a particularly monstrous quality and I walked through it in large sweeping strides toward the gate. Hardly any moon. Past the gate was unfamiliar, as if the high wall had been shattered and taken out of its place, along with the trees and the marsh, all of it scorched and shifted as though there had been a large earthquake.

No stars.

The woods were thick with pitch and my feet got sucked into large patches of mud. I was trying to get back to the road, get a car? I walked clumsily through brush, reeds snapping beneath me, until I reached a clearing.

There stood a large dark shape in the center of the empty field. It was tall and angry, shapeless like a chimera. The shape stayed still, though it felt like it was roving and pulsing, pursuing me from all sides, until I found myself approaching it and standing beside it. The form rose and towered like a large tree. I was suddenly its shadow and it lowered onto me, pushing me onto the ground, pressing at me like black fire. The form was so enormous that I felt as though I was crushed into a room of a dark house, or that I had been dug deep under the earth to hide from the moon like some sort of wretched person made of mud—small, and tired, and ever so insoluble.

My senses came on, one by one. Cold soil. Wet log. Some shaking leaves in a passing breeze. Gunpowder mouth. Dull headache. A slug on my leg. Latent fog. A golden sun. I was curled up in the clearing near the swamp outside the house.

But I didn't feel heavy.

I got up and picked the leaves off my skirt and looked around for my wall. I didn't see it. I didn't worry. I walked a few steps out from the marsh and looked again and saw the gate between trees.

The gate had closed in the night so I had to climb the vines. Step by step I scaled the wall until I ungracefully perched at the top of the wall and looked.

The rising sun was stuck in a low stretch of fog, filling the entire patch of property to make a solid flash of orange. Rays that broke through the fog were contained in strands of mist, creating floating red and fuchsia patches, and when I looked up, way high, high there, was a heron. Another planet had emerged out of the ugly, frightening one I had encountered the night before, and I brought my eyes down to meet it.

There was no more food left in the cupboards or the pantry. Much of my stress was now from the body; whatever emotional duress I was originally experiencing was now impossible to see or do anything about. I walked again, exhausted. In the daytime, the path was easy to navigate. Clear.

I found my way to a main road, where I had been weeks ago.

The train station was a small brick building, beside it a post office, beside it a market and so on. A town.

At the market I got eggs, rice, tomatoes, onions, milk, lemons, a loaf. Simple foods. I felt as if I was covered in tight casts and bandages. I bought a small red wagon, the kind that children use to lug each other around. I placed my bag of simple foods in it and walked out into the sun again.

On the sidewalk, I retrieved sourdough bread from the wagon and took large pulling bites. Swallowed them quickly. A young girl, chewing gum, and her father watched me from their car. I resisted throwing the nubby loaf at their windshield. I walked down the street in the wrong direction, too nervous to turn around.

I reached a line of trees at the end of the block. The trees were single file, straight and flat, and latticed together to form a fence. Their complex weaving excited me. I imagined someone spending years leading and pruning the branches until the pattern was fully formed. All of life is like this, I considered. My life could be like this. Fruits hung from the branches!

Through the branches was a gardener in neon boots, singing a melody in a major key. NURSERY was written on a sign, tacked onto a small wooden building behind him. I went inside while almost regretting it, pushing down the desire to be closed away in the cottage.

Inside were more neat rows. Rows of herbs and tropical plants, vegetables and hanging baskets. And through the back door were lines of trees, similar to the ones out front.

The thought of some fruit trees at the property felt stirring, if not a sign of something purposeful, so I selected a single pear tree sapling, crooked with small leaves. The singing gardener in neon boots rang me up at the register. Up close he looked like an old hippie, and he asked if I knew of Donovan or Cat Stevens. I muttered a reply and he gave me leaflets that explained orchard growing, perennial care, and other things. I thanked him, so overwhelmed by his casual kindness that I almost teared up while placing the small crooked pear tree into my red wagon.

I was leaving the nursery when I heard a faint collection of voices. I climbed up the hill with my red wagon, following the sounds, until I reached an old Congregational church. The pear tree inspired some sort of valiance in me, proving some capability, so when I experienced a curiosity toward the chapel and the music, my body unthinkingly carried me forward—the way one's feet continuously navigate across a scramble of rocks—through the front doors. The tall, skinny windows were propped open with umbrellas and inside smelled like math textbooks. I slipped into a pew in the back with a woman who handed me a red book. I had left my wagon outside but brought in the pear sapling, and seated it on the pew beside me. All around, women and men sang a hymn that I thought I'd heard before, and out the windows hemlocks bent and swayed across the grove.

A man with large white hair sat in the pew in front of me; a green caterpillar inched across the back of his collar. At the end of the hymn he stood up and climbed the stairs to the pulpit. The chapel was so old that creaks shuttered across the floor like lightning.

In the beginning was the . . . he said. I relaxed, so overfamiliar with the phrase that it inconsequentially floated past me.

I tried to remember the last time I was in church. Perhaps when I visited my mother, before moving across the country. There, in the old pew, my attention drifted as

I looked out the window. When I turned back, the green caterpillar was creeping into the preacher's hair.

Words don't fall away and disappear, but form thought shapes, lead separate lives . . . blossom, or echo, clicking into meaning years later . . .

I touched my leg.

Revelation finds its time . . . The preacher's hair looked stiffly bent. *The things you say can either build and lift something up, or produce a rot—not only in those who hear, but in you too.*

I imagined his words as small, buoyant pearls, cast from the front of the chapel and out the propped-open windows, into the town, over the house and the high wall, some falling and settling onto the ground, falling into open windows of parked cars outside the market or into the potted soil at the nursery, breathed in and carried on clothes, waiting to be encountered and revealed. I imagined all our words living out similar courses, so that we were moving through a misty network of word droplets, which changed in concentration and motivation depending on the proximity of certain people and ideas, and how easily the tide of language might be manipulated by propagating our tongues and hearts with goodness, by choosing to say and repeat it.

Eventually the pews emptied out and I stayed, quiet and calm, vaguely recalling Psalms—*My God, I cry out by day, but you do not answer.*

A woman reentered the church to retrieve her glasses case. She looked up at me, surprised. On the way out, she paused at my pew.

"It looks like you had a good day," she said, referring to the pear tree. We both smiled. She placed her hand on my shoulder for a moment, then wished me goodnight.

I walked back, pulling my red wagon. The clouds stretched across the sky and I had a hard time seeing the path, so I walked slowly with my arm outstretched, touching nothing or touching a leaf on a branch, then shifting and recalibrating myself. The trees towered so high that they blocked out any moonlight that could have helped me adjust to the dark.

Occasionally I'd bump into a branch and would be surprised by how soft it was. For an hour I walked the path. The forest transformed into something halcyon and storybook-like, as though the many creatures were guiding me along with a gentle touch, like a small caterpillar rounding around on skin.

Before deciding where to put the pear tree, I did what I so often watched my mother do. In the morning she'd look at where the sun was and sketch the shadows, the same in the afternoon, the same in late afternoon, evening. She had a notebook of shadow maps, of different rooms and views of the yard. Imprints, traces, impressions, marks, and stains of things. A tree's shadow moved from left to right. The shadow of a ceiling fan was a long pressed daisy. Footprints and furniture silhouettes. My mother could tell the time based on any room and its shadows within a ten-minute window of accuracy. Shadow-mapping felt to her like observing the unknown side of visible things. Forgotten until focused on, and meaningless unless questioned, like a watermark, a trail of cologne, or kicked-up road dust behind a lone driver. As mothers often do, she saw something I couldn't yet see. I stood outside with the bright sun behind me and copied my form. It was the reaching, fleeting version of me.

I dug a hole in the clay soil. An orange cat came and kept me company. In the morning I found that it left gifts in the hole I dug. My back ached and I read the gardener's pamphlets and returned to town to buy aged horse manure, then mixed it into the soil so that the pear tree would have nutrients. At the internet's suggestion, I planted comfrey in places where the ground needed drainage and Austrian winter peas to put nitrogen into the soil. I wondered what the opposite of living limerently was, how to snub the desire to be where and who I was not. I figured out the lawn mower, sat outside and tanned in the sun while scrubbing the fountain back to white.

The pear sapling was some yoke of anxiety for me. If it lived in my care, then other things would too, but if not, then nothing would. Thus went my logic. There seemed to be two ways of living that I'd encountered up until that point. The first was foreign to me and seemed to be possessed by phlegmatic individuals, and involved starting many projects, planting many seeds, and knocking on many doors, openly accepting invitations and pursuing any and every innovation one desired within reason, with the calm understanding that some efforts wouldn't fully succeed. The second tendency, which I had the most experience with, involved a careful investigation of every effort, weighing its possible setbacks, which were always infinite, and moving forward only if it had promised a precise and sure success. In this second approach, anxiety meant succumbing to a hyperawareness of possibility, so that nearly nothing emerged into the realm of the real.

I considered whether faking the first way of living would allow me to learn it. The sapling, with its delicate crookedness and my limited pear tree–caretaking abilities, seemed to ask me to try.

I returned to the nursery again, this time buying many fruit tree saplings. Apple, sour cherry, persimmon, pawpaw, plum, fig, olive. This way, I'll increase my chances of success, I considered. The singing gardener, who laughed with his eyes closed when I told him that I wanted to plant thirty trees, helped me blueprint the locations for the first few. He pointed out the species that were everbearing and self-pollinating, and I filled my red wagon with them.

In the mornings I tried humming the melodies from a dusty hymnal tucked beneath the couch in the living room. There was a handwritten inscription in the front cover that said, "But I am a worm, and no man . . . my heart . . . like wax . . ." The rest was splotchy and indiscernible, as if smudged by tears or rain.

I enjoyed the digging. The spade pushing through a hard place and breaking it into pieces. Bringing up dirt, brick, stones. Occasionally I hoped to find an artifact, like an old license plate or a glass bottle. My back ached; I had pain in parts of my legs that I'd never felt, so in the evening I opened my laptop and looked for more effective ways to dig. I watched an excited Irish woman on YouTube dig a hole correctly, and I mimicked her movements in the living room like a rusty dancer. I took note of how to use my body more efficiently: energy from the legs and core, instead of the back.

While I practiced outside I listened to an interview with a psychologist who talked about how bereaved children used sandboxes to process grief. They'd hide objects in the sand—toys, sparkly bouncy balls, figurines—and with their plastic shovels search and bring them up again. They practiced uncovering something that had been lost.

For days I woke up with the sun and dug. My clothes were stained with red dirt and I took long breaks; feeling high from exertion, I sat up against the fountain with a glass of lemon water. The tips of branches shifted above the high wall. The blue heron inched across the pond.

It felt as if I was taking steps straight into the sea, but as soon as my step passed the surface of the water, a stone would rise up to meet my feet. Occasionally I looked up and saw that I was led forward, but at the same time, I woke up each morning with the distinct feeling of having to start again from the beginning.

Those were blissful days. I lived as if I was living permanently, in a place where I was only temporary.

The dwarf trees wouldn't bear fruit for another few years, but when I looked upon them, newly planted in the ground, I imagined them in their full heights, with gleaming yields—plums, pears, olives. The thought of someone I'd never met, or Simone—whom I haven't seen in years—finding the orchard made me giddy, but on other days it made me wish that I had never come here in the first place, and instead was living in a cold insensitive place, like a high-rise apartment along a busy metropolis, someplace that I could disappear even to myself. It was the dreary line between responsibility and fear, and I wanted in those moments to be punished, a sterile room with a wall of thick glass to look out at the dirt and the city, constant rain, pills and bottles of champagne. I imagined the man from Walby Point entering through the door, twisting me like the roots of a crab apple tree.

This was a limerence for another world that destroyed all joy. I began calling it "limes" as some lovely-dumb nickname. Some days I was "heavy with limes," and more and more days I had none, or one that I could easily throw into the pond.

The area around the property proved to be quite plentiful. Many of the vines bore grapes, and the swamp area and woods were lush with chicken of the woods and chanterelle mushrooms, St. John's wort, echinacea, plantain leaves for salad, and white raspberries—sweeter than other berries and resembling frosted glass. I went on walks with plant identification books that I found in the cottage. The empty field where I had experienced my dark night was not quite empty anymore but full of information and names, uses, properties, and potentials, with palaces of underground burrows and pathways beneath the surface. Loud *sh-shhh*s, *cccrrrk*s, *thmp*s, *szun-szun-szun* of flapping, *jjjjsseejjjjj* of buzzing . . . if I stayed in the field long enough I could hear the plants stretching and growing, creaking as they drooped in sleep at the end of light. I saw something reflected in myself too, a space inside becoming three-dimensional, an unknown shape gaining gleam.

My last days there were also the last days of summer. Simone wrote to remind me when she'd be returning to the house. I felt a great dismay, fearing that this new surging would disappear again. Maybe I'd secretly been expecting her to change her mind, or maybe I had forgotten to expect things at all. Now I had to do something, yet all I could think of was death or Death Valley Junction. Not even nature, in its stillness and silence, could pull me out of myself in any lasting way. Even after days when I was grateful to be surrounded by its complexity and beauty, and would experience weightlessness and relief, I would still retreat, hours later, within my rattled body, unable to bring nature inside. I turned to face myself and it failed. There was still a door in me, and I kept it shut.

Many of the flowers had withered. The leaves were beginning to shed, and a hush fell over the cottage and the property. I anticipated the feeling of being an eternal outsider, some forever homesickness, as I spent the day packing my things in the rollaway luggage and buying a plane ticket online.

I worked all through the night putting together the grandest meal I'd ever made—rabbit stew with mushrooms, sweet braised lamb dumplings, red cabbage with apples and dill, and a French peach pie. The meal kept warm on the stove, and I set the table for one, with a thank-you note for Simone on the plate. For a moment the house felt warm and lived in; I could almost hear music and murmuring in the next room.

I stood outside by the fountain as the sun rose, then walked among the fruit trees to say goodbye to each. The saplings were so frail. I wondered what would happen to them. The crooked pear tree had a new leaf, bright green.

After I tidied the house, I tasted the stew. Ladled some into the bowl and ate it slowly, as if I was Simone. Instead of washing the spoon, I ladled more. Something defiant and familiar unfurled within me and I continued, desiring more even as the next spoonful reached my mouth. I had never made something so lavish. Reaching the bottom of the pot, I left a scatter of gristle and wet stems, and swiftly moved on to the dumplings, smothering them in cabbage and dill. I gasped for air while swallowing. The flavor was so rich that I laughed and ate more of the tender meat, feeling like I wasn't able to get a bite satisfying enough, craving even while I was getting what I was craving, and with each dumpling dreading its end.

Then there was the pie, uncut and glossed. It was so soft and filled with cream.

I polished off the pie tin, and left quickly, still hungry, before Simone arrived.

3

The rental assistant gave me a white convertible. He winked and jangled the keys before handing them to me. What did he think a lone woman did in the desert?

"I'm looking for someone," I said.

He looked through a file folder.

I put my luggage—containing clothes, a book on trees, and a Bible I found on a shelf in Simone's cottage—on the passenger seat. I drove out of the airport complex and down US 160 with a broken radio. I followed the same road for miles, attempting a prayer. *Thank you* . . .

The scenery made me parched. My tongue tacked to the top of my mouth. I found a pack of Turkish cigarettes tucked in the glove compartment. Stale. At one point they had been wet; now they smelled like golden raisins. A headache flushed around my eyes.

The same glimpse again and again: light sand, washed-out cacti, low curves in the distance, light sand, washed-out cacti, low curves in the distance, light sand, washed-out cacti, low curves in the distance.

A giant wooden cow stood in the sand beside a parking lot, and ducks decidedly approached me, expecting bread, as I dangled a leg out of the car. I had stopped for water at a fueling station on a stretched road.

The place felt like a wasteland wunderkammer: inside the building were meteorites in glass cases, a generator formerly used to power the entire town, cowboy paintings and trinkets, a quick-mart selling soft drinks and switchblades disguised as lipstick. There was also a saloon, a chapel, and upstairs, an empty steakhouse.

The building, as well as its longer-distance neighbor Las Vegas, was Victorian in its amassed curios, as if it emerged out of a panic in response to the desert's blankness.

The person at the register smiled and patted a bloated white cat. A sheriff and two older men eyed me as I bought a gallon jug of water. I waved at them, then steadily walked back to the car.

My mother would record herself with a pocket tape recorder on long car trips, to "strengthen my verbal IQ." The exercise would inevitably involve her, unsure of what to say, speaking, seemingly at random, about things she remembered, until she grew tired.

I spoke into the voice recorder app on my phone: I'm five feet six, black hair, left-handed . . . angels have six wings . . . quills were once made of goose feathers . . . I can make a whistle out of a long piece of grass . . . I once fixed my therapist's flat tire outside the office in order to put off going to my appointment . . . there are maps for only 10 to 15 percent of ocean floors . . . my favorite movie is *Babette's Feast* . . . grapefruits lower your blood pressure and in my friend's home country an entire community was sedated during a summer of a heavy grapefruit crop . . . I wonder what Simone will think of the fruit trees on her property . . . I long for a family again . . . black walnut trees grow in the direction of other black walnut trees . . . Peter in middle school was in a religious choir and would travel across Europe with a saint's embalmed hand—he'd barely sleep during the trip in fear of it coming back to life to find him . . . I dream of places more than people, mansions in muted colors, long glass hallways with rivers at either side . . . if God exists outside of time does everything in the world happen at once? I babysat a third grader who was obsessed with Pascal's wager—he kept a notebook filled with illustrations of cartoonish characters with "Pascal's Wager" written beneath them . . .

I let the recorder continue as I fell quiet. I imagined the convertible as a flicked coin paused midair. I couldn't make *the decision*, the *defining step*, toward belief, I thought . . . I felt the God-doubt press at me more and more. When I'd asked the third grader who God was, he'd said it was his friend, Mr. Moon, the orchestra conductor who lived in a crater and conducted us all.

I wondered where my mother was and imagined her pushing a cart through a grocery store, handling produce, deciding which register to go to depending on which cashier looked loneliest. I imagined her locking her car when she got home, balancing her grocery bags as she walked up the front steps. She wore a blue cardigan, and the socks with little flowers on them that I always used to borrow.

I put my car window down and let my fingers ride the wind, until I saw buildings take shape at the horizon.

Dust devils and dirt. A skulking cloud.

There it was, the Amargosa Hotel and Opera House, just like in pictures, a little more worn with patina.

I stared from the car, finishing up the gallon jug.

For a moment the wind, a measureless white noise, surged and overcame itself like an ocean wave. A surfer once told me that all the rushing water sounds fade away when you are gliding through barrel waves. In the center of chaos is a stillness where people forget where they are.

I massaged my neck, stiff from the drive.

At first, I couldn't bring myself to go inside, so I got out of the car and explored the junction instead. I stepped around the opera house and remnants of a rail yard, over bush cacti and cakes of wild horse manure.

Tamarisk tree branches dangled over the junction like green curtains. A small sign stood beside them, indicating that they were invasive and have a behemothic thirst—two hundred gallons of water from the ground per day, all the moisture from the air at night—but in the searing daytime heat, the water evaporates from the tree and cools in its shade.

The tamarisk trees wove around the junction between the abandoned sheds and buildings. Their soft needles littered the ground. I spotted a sparrow trapped in mid-flight between two panes of glass, caught as someone was opening or closing the window. Wings intact and spread like a pressed flower.

Having mustered up the courage, I rounded to the front

again to the entrance of the hotel, and looked at the peeling white paint accented with blue letters across the front. I imagined that Marta had requested that I meet her at the junction in order to consume me. But the beckoning didn't feel like it was from Marta. All I knew was that I needed to be there, for a showdown with something unknown to me, before something brilliant could happen.

I entered the hotel, into a silent lobby.

A ticking clock. I stood on red carpet.

On the wall was a trompe l'oeil of Death Valley Junction, painted in warm terra-cotta and sand tones. The mural depicted a different version than the one I was just circling. Here, the opera house and hotel were in ruins. Tall colonnades with de Chirico–type shadows remained against beige mountains, and a spiraling dust fluttered above like a halo.

A white silhouette of a ballet dancer was faintly traced in the sky.

The focal point of the lobby was a portrait of Marta on the mantel of the fireplace beside the trompe l'oeil; her eyes met me across the room. She wore a tiara, looked like a princess.

A woman to the side of the mural cleared her throat.

I apologized for not noticing her, and explained that I had booked a room for a few days. She checked me in and noted that the water was finicky. As she rummaged through a drawer for my key, I shared that I was on leave from my job, and that I'd always wanted to visit because I was drawn to Marta and studied her life. The woman held the key out across the counter and dropped it clumsily. I picked it up. Together we walked down the hallway. Frames and portraits were painted on the hallway wall.

The floor was craterous. My steps sank into the red carpet in unexpected places.

"The tamarisk roots," the receptionist said despairingly

when I tripped on a raised part in the carpet. "They're breaking apart the foundation. . . . They're so long that they've gone to the center of the earth and back up again to uproot the place."

She asked if I needed any toiletries, then left me at my room.

The room was marked by a musky vegetal smell, similar to ambergris, a calcified whale bile used in perfumes that I occasionally smelled on Peter's friends or women in museum gift shops. The pink curtains cast pink light. I sat down on the bed and felt a weary excitement, then thirst.

Marta had painted stretched acrobats and trapeze artists across the ceiling and walls.

I stood, reaching my arms up and stretching my legs.

In the bathroom was a pyramid-style skylight that framed the dusk. The bathroom mirror was matted with a beige dust and I wet a spot to peer through. I too was silty, wrinkling, and odd.

Keen to wander, I left my pink room and walked back down the red carpet of the portrait hallway. At the end of the hallway and through the lobby was a dining room where three individuals convened around a small circular table.

I paused behind the archway, listening briefly before deciding whether to enter the room. I made out the phrase *Marta would have wanted* and some mutterings about costumes. In the center of the table was a flickering white candle.

I crouched down in the corner to observe.

The speakers were three women. All dressed in blue. One with intense eyes behind circle glasses, another with a long bent neck. The third peeled an orange, ate it, segment by segment, followed by the peel.

It became apparent—based on the way people talk when they talk about money and property—that they were responsible for the junction. "The preservationists," as one referred to themselves, parsed through what needed to be done about the opera house.

I debated whether or not to reveal myself. I could ask them questions about Marta. I could step out from behind the archway and ask what their names were. But before I could move into sight, they finished their conversation and bid each other goodnight, as though sensing that they were being watched. One by one, they stood up. They were frighteningly tall and the gust from their movements caused the candle to blow out. Passing me, they walked through the hallway and out into the darkness.

A story one preservationist told to another:

A paratrooper in training drops onto the airstrip behind the Amargosa Hotel. As he folds up his parachute he sees a woman in a black dress and a straw hat, slender with an hourglass waist untouched by childbirth, approach.

"Who the hell are you?" he says to her, full of adrenaline and wind.

"Who the hell are you!" she shouts back.

The paratrooper tells her his name, "I just jumped out of an airplane, I'm about to run twenty miles," he says.

"I'm Marta Becket, and this is *my town*."

During the day, the preservationists scattered across the property, mining Marta's old things. In the evenings they gathered in the dining room with their findings and stories, their lists of financiers and projects. I pieced together that they were there for the week to decide what to do with the property, and whether the hotel brought in enough money to maintain the basic operations.

"It's hanging on a gossamer thread," one whispered urgently.

Like a dance, the opera house pirouetted. With a flash of tulle dared to be gone.

Meanwhile, I played the part of an off-the-clock detective, seeking something, attending to clues. Whenever it felt like I was escaping myself into the remnants of Marta's vibrant world, just as she flew away from New York into the desert, I returned to the anchoring zone of my pink room to stretch, or read a Psalm, or write things down.

A man sat on the sofa in the lobby. He was looking at the trompe l'oeil mural of the ruins, and wore a loose-fitting gray suit. His red hair slicked back.

He said hello, slightly louder than one usually does. I laughed. He smiled wide. He slid down the couch for me to sit. The couch upholstery was an itchy burlap on my bare legs. I smelled the ambergris again, faintly.

"What do you think?" he asked, pointing at the mural of the Amargosa Opera House in ruins.

I paused for a moment, crossing then uncrossing my legs. "It's either this place one hundred years ago, or in a hundred years?" I looked over at him, raising my eyebrows in a kind of faux seriousness.

He nodded. There was a large mole on his cheekbone, and he possessed a lucid, accomplished demeanor of someone who had walked a great distance. Almost misplaced at the hotel, as if he had arrived by chance. A jolly tourist in a fading town. His suit had a shimmering quality to it. I wondered if it felt like silk.

I asked the jolly tourist where he was from, and he explained in his amplified voice that he was a travel agent. "For decades," he said, waving his hands like he was waving away the years. He wasn't a trapped man, but part of himself had definitely been carved out, in order to roll over the world like a pilgrim, never married, no surviving family, looking past the people he'd meet in anticipation of what lay ahead. For so long, he thought in terms of someone else's leisure, bookings, rooms with views, weather reports. But when he entered early retirement he couldn't imagine what else to do besides continue, so he became his own client. He leaned forward on the sofa and beckoned me closer. I scooted to the edge and he pointed back at the painted ruins.

"There's a mural at the Trinità dei Monti convent—it's anamorphic," he explained, using wide hand gestures. "At first, it seems to be a landscape stretching along the hallway. You see a field, some woods, little shepherds. But, you walk further down the hallway, and reach a precise moment in perspective where the image turns into St. Paul praying beneath a tree.

"A few steps further, and it's a landscape again. A few steps back, and it's St. Paul. A little, or big, secret in plain sight," he said.

"For a moment it's there, and then it's gone," I offered.

"Gone, no! It's always there, and always was," he said, laughing wildly, "but there's always someone stuck looking at the landscape," he added gravely.

I laughed, charmed.

The world was covered in pinholes to be peered in. Ideas emerging in precise places, containing endless opportunities for revelation. Speckling the landscape, scattered in people, and projected into the things they made and said. Marta and her husband could have left the broken-down trailer sixty years ago and walked past the small pinhole in one of the doors at Death Valley Junction. Missing it, she would never have seen the empty theater with its warped stage and kangaroo rats and torn curtains.

I closed my left eye and pretended that I was looking at the junction in the past, then opened it and closed my right eye, pretending that I was looking at the junction far into the future, after some apocalypse when the sun fell from the sky. I blinked, rapidly switching my eyes, as the image oscillated forward and backward in time, forward and backward between different paths and possibilities, between two sides of ruin, as I used to live—forward and backward—between the despairing antipossibility of my past, and the possible despair in my future. My past as a dejected lonely child of lonely people, and the future of a life alone. The past-future seesaw was suddenly so obviously nauseating to me that the room began to spin.

I turned to the jolly tourist. He was no longer there.

I checked the hallway, then walked outside, but couldn't find him.

Across the junction was the opera house.

The doors were blocked by large orange sandbags and secured with padlocks and chains. I imagined some sort of vortex within, a bridge to a further realm that needed to be guarded. I wondered if I'd see Marta again, walking through the dust. Traveling slowly, fighting the wind.

"Hello?" I called.

Nothing.

"Rats," I muttered.

I walked back into the hotel and passed an empty water glass I had abandoned. I picked it up and continued past the cardboard cutouts of dancers, locking eyes with Marta's portraits. I was beginning to feel uncomfortable. I didn't know what I was doing there, held again above the surface of a bottomless expanse.

What felt real in this dollhouse in the desert were things I couldn't see. A prayer felt stark and concrete, full of movement, like a kicking in the belly. I felt a tug toward God both in me like a speck of pollen, and outside me like a meadow, propagated by my mother's many words that drifted around my life like pearls.

Unsure of how to begin a prayer, I'd turn to a random page in one of my books and read what was before me. I ran over the words like a metal detector, until something caught me.

Do not lay up for yourselves treasures on earth, where moth and rust destroy and where thieves break in and steal, but lay up for yourselves treasures in heaven . . . for where your treasure is, there your heart will also be.

I looked upon the words *moth and rust* and repeated them in my mind until they settled in me somewhere. I longed for something untouched by moth and rust.

I was surprised to come across the tamarisk trees in Genesis 21:33, as a promise: *Then Abraham planted a tamarisk tree in Beersheba, and there called on the name of the Lord, the Everlasting God.*

I'd sit in the pink room of the hotel, reading the Gospels,

nondescriptly mumbling into my hands. Other times, I prayed straightforwardly about piecemeal things of no consequence, like the heat in Death Valley, or a sore muscle.

I felt like I was constantly turning toward something out of the corner of my eye.

What followed each prayer was silence, then desire or frustration. Sometimes I didn't feel anything. Each ended with the same plea, awkwardly. *God.*

My mother had mentioned that when she started praying, she felt her defenses torn down in shreds. She moved to America and was robbed at gunpoint at a gas station for all the money she had, pregnant with me at eight months. Something beneath the world was thrashing at her faith's footing, and was trying its best to knock the balance.

The next night, I returned to the dining room. The preservationists sat around the table. Lights off. Candles flickering. The evening was more intimate and elusive than the last time I had seen them. Again, I couldn't bring myself to approach them.

I backed behind the archway, crouching down.

They were talking about the overlap of the *two Toms*. The first, Marta's husband, lost to brothels. The second Tom, or as Marta called him, Wilget, was the maintenance man, who used to speed around in a go-kart and dance with tools in the shed.

Marta, fond of Wilget, eventually asked him to be the master of ceremonies at her performances, and on his first night on the job, Marta's husband set a small fire behind House Ten of the junction and drove away forever. I imagined the flames licking the side of the white adobe building. The new Tom entered onto the stage and replaced the old Tom. One set fire to things while the other mended them. He willingly stepped into Marta's pulsing world and put on a hoop skirt in the process. He made miniature railroads that laced around the junction, and a music machine constructed of many instruments. Finally, instead of solos there were duets. Marta had a friend.

The new Tom died of a stroke, leaving Marta in her final years. The preservationists found some documentation of the performances that followed Wilget's absence, and mourned how heartbreaking it was to see her dance around the empty chair.

The preservationists continued talking, *the future the future the future*. The flickering candle illuminated the creeping cracks on the walls, a dusty webbiness to the corners of the ceiling, and the shattered lamp in the corner of the room.

That evening a terrible clanging persisted at the window in the pink room. When I glanced toward the night, I thought I saw the large formless shadow appear to me again, approaching the pane. This time I got up from bed and unlatched the window. I took a box of matches and lit the candle at the sill. The shadow trembled and was driven out. When I closed the window, a rare, lush rain began to fall.

I awoke the next morning, slumped against the mattress, still wearing my shoes and my red dress from the day before. My hair was smoothed and clipped. The door and windows were locked and I checked beneath the bed and behind the shower curtain but found only a dried-up scorpion.

Beside my bed was another empty water glass. I stumbled into the bathroom to turn on the faucet but no water came out, neither from the sink nor from the shower. When I twisted the knob it snapped off into my hand. The tiles around it shattered and crumbled into the tub, revealing a twisted tamarisk root pushing through the wall.

I took the convertible down the state line toward Death Valley National Park. Passed through Zabriskie Point, a rippling vista of clay, volcanic ash, and petrified sand. Imagined what it must have been like to be the first person to encounter it. I saw nothing, no water, not even a cactus, only blistering forms and two young boys crouched at the side of the road, cracking eggs onto the sand to watch them cook. In the 1950s a new kind of entertainment—which involved standing on a platform in the desert with flimsy tinted goggles as mushroom clouds ballooned into the sky—emerged in Las Vegas. Some saw the nuclear tests from their hotel windows or while riding the bus. So many tickets were sold, so many atomic bombs exploded, that some later speculated the results were threefold to Chernobyl. The desert's bareness buzzed with buried, secret things.

I drove until I reached Badwater, the lowest point in the country. I was the only person on the planet at this large bare base of husked stone. Extraterrestrial rock formations stretched out in the distance. The ground was crusted with a thin sheet of salt. I walked out onto the flat expanse until I felt far enough from my car. At a seemingly arbitrary spot, I stood entirely still.

Thousands of years ago, a hundred miles of water covered where I stood. Melted ice from the Sierra Nevadas brought in enough water to fill a lake that was six hundred feet deep. When it all dried up, deposits rich with salt and borate were left behind. From verdance and natural wealth to dry heat and human industry. The world was constantly rearranging itself. Scientists have drilled far into the ice sheets of Antarctica to find fossils of subtropical rainforests, palm trees, macadamia nuts. New movements constantly emerged.

Here I was, attempting, again, my meager prayer.

I waited a few minutes, then began again, urgently this time, reaching high out of myself, and in the stretching, I felt something hover over me.

A most present thing occurred, like a flare, all flame, from all sides. A presence shook me; it was strong and wild, shattering enough to place at the front of something.

There on the flat expanse, surrounded by brutal rising mountains, I was awash in what felt like a mix of terror and grace. I became small and unnoticeable, but it was a smallness where something wonderful surged around me. The smaller I became, the more I could see it. Like a fractaling reveal, tying my days together with a single thread. I crinkled down onto the sand.

I felt the squint that happens when one is staring directly into the sun, but it was my entire body squinting at love.

After a long moment, I walked, soundlessly, across the flat ground back to my car. I drove slow through the mountains with the windows open.

I was surrounded by emptiness, and didn't wish to fill it.

I ambled back into the lobby, flush-faced. The shock turned to ecstatic giddiness. Who could I tell this to? I thought. God's touch! Everything else in comparison was gray-washed. The mycelium of heaven, beneath everything, making small plush things grow from din.

The preservationists weren't in the dining room. Instead, their things were scattered across the table.

Piles of papers, Marta's sketches, poetry, unpaid taxes, playbills. I couldn't resist: I sat down and lightly touched the papers, moving them around like a magic trick. Worn plastic wineglasses. I was reading a pamphlet that must have at one point been sold at the gift shop—

> I do not plan for the years ahead. I don't try to attempt to guess what I will be able to do ten years from now. At present, I dance, and I continue to paint. I dare not question where I go from here. I do not predict big plans for my art and the town of Death Valley Junction. Instead . . . I work. I do the best I can.

—when I heard the sound of slow footsteps shortly behind me.

Blue fabric swishing like waves.

For a moment we simply looked at one another. Me and the preservationists. Silently detecting motivation. Belligerent scenarios popped into my head. What if I shook them by the shoulders, asking them if they'd heard of Christ like a cartoonish born-again? What if I threw money at them? I scratched the side of my neck.

I calmly apologized for sifting through their things. I told them why I was there. One of them smiled. They had noticed me before, roaming around the junction, taking notes. The preservationists had soft, foggy voices. Relief and nervousness prickled through me. There are often visitors who walk through the hotel after weary days, they said, who wouldn't even notice the opera house sign outside their window. People were drawn to the place because it looked as if it had its share of ghosts, and they thought maybe if they were lucky enough they could post something to their social media account—some sound or eerie flicker of light. How bankrupt and twice-dead those ideas of ghosts were, they said, compared to the "waning ghost of individual ingenuity."

Often, people tried to keep the wrong things alive, or kept things alive in the wrong ways. I too had tried to preserve myself, but the object of preservation can never be the one to do the preserving. Life comes from outside of time.

They weren't entirely certain how they found themselves preserving Marta's legacy, they said. We were sitting at the table then. At one point they had worked for her, and even before then, something had caught them the moment they met Marta. They couldn't help coming back.

Marta had asked one of them to take her place in one of the evening performances. For days she studied Marta, trying her best to copy her movements. When the stage curtains opened that night, the preservationist-in-making looked out at the painted audience and for a moment felt that she truly had become Marta, with direct access to a complete other world.

Maybe she did. She no longer remembered that performance at all, she said. The memory was out of reach behind a locked door.

That magnetic realm. Marta's final performance was called the "Sitting Down Show," and Marta danced, moving her legs ever so slightly, from her wheelchair, while in her mind she flitted back and forth across the stage.

Only a small part of the preservation work was keeping her together through artifacts. Her paintings, costumes, compositions, letters. The crown jewel—the opera house. All of it, her life in objects, could be gone in a moment, through flood or fire, and they knew that well. Time wins over time.

What survives materiality is a story.

The jolly tourist sat on a patio chair beside the front doors to the opera house. He waved as we approached. Pale and tall, with slicked-back red hair, his gray suit. With a wink to me, he asked if we were giving tours.

I was overjoyed. He seemed sunny, unbothered—a combination of qualities that made me aware of my seriousness. My shoulders relaxed and my hands slipped into my dress pockets. Even the preservationists seemed stiff by comparison. They nodded, and said that officially tours had stopped due to finances, but they were happy to have him along.

Together we moved the orange sandbags from the door, and the preservationists untangled the chains.

Stepping into the opera house I became even more aware of myself, of the room, some kismet. Everything emerged at once as the doors closed behind us.

The coffee-can lights switched on and everyone fell quiet.

The preservationists took out their flashlights and ran the beams across the illustrated audience on the walls, referring to it as "the Sistine Chapel of the United States."

I moved slowly, following the flashlights across the wall, watching the hand-painted faces—nuns, prostitutes, noblemen, Marta's cat with a litter of kittens—light up in turn. The beam stopped at a figure with a long sword and costume, without a face.

One preservationist chuckled, and, referring to the smudged face, explained how people promised to fund her opera house, and in return Marta would paint them somewhere in the junction. Occasionally they'd fail to pay up, so Marta would paint over their faces in murky gold paint, or erase them entirely.

The place seemed bigger and smaller than I expected it to be, with deep pigments and a sweeping ceiling fresco of the Muses that left me quiet with my neck craned back. I walked slowly down the aisle and took everything in, unsure of how to be, walking up onto the stage timidly, leaving the jolly tourist and the preservationists.

To the side of the stage were various hand-painted curtains. I reached to touch them. They were old and unopened for a long while and the paint crumbled in my fingertips. I held the corner then let it go. I was saddled with a mix of stillness and wait. It was almost as if I had visited a photograph of the place, or was looking at the image of a star in the sky that had already come to pass.

The opera house was bitterly beautiful, with part of its beauty elsewhere. I used to find comfort in the idea of a forest made of plywood, my life made into a set, because it was a resemblance of a life, without a life in it—no celebration nor pain, no responsibility nor desire. Sometimes serenity and purgatory wear the same face.

Behind the curtains was a steep staircase. I climbed, and at the top I reached a dark, unadorned room above the stage, with bare plywood walls and a chair tipped onto its side. Neither windows nor colors. The room was like a place for hiding, sealed off from the rest of the theater.

I sat in the chair and rested. I considered whether Marta

loved her audience, or whether she wanted it to love her; if in her performances she was willfully brushing away some anxiety, absence, abyss; if, in that room, that cramped dim room above her stage, she questioned if it could happen, as I've so often done in my own room—if she could uphold a vision of herself to the world. Even Lucifer was a beautiful angel once, close to God, talented and wise, fully aware of how resplendent love could be, before deciding that he wanted to make a go of it on his own, dance his own dances in his own house of games.

I thanked God for bringing me there, to show me the place I'd been so drawn to.

And with that, things felt as if they had reached their natural end. I had turned over the details of the opera house for so long that to *visit it* became an act of remembering, the act of remembering an act of forgetting, the act of forgetting an active motion. I descended from the attic.

Downstairs, the jolly tourist turned circles in the aisle between chairs, pointing and shouting.

The tourist shouted about the image of jesters. Laughing, he exclaimed that he had had no idea that the theater existed, and that he arrived on a recommendation from the neighboring town that it would be a good place to see a ghost. He was surprised at its beauty and remarkable life, and for a moment I envied his being able to see it all at once for the first time.

The preservationists frowned. I had previously seen them as gentle, but in that light they took on acerbic faces.

One preservationist pointed the flashlight to the ceiling, where a crack had caused a leak to run down the side of the audience mural. She pointed her flashlight to the lights that had begun to rust, then to a dead rat beneath a chair, and then directly upon the face of the jolly tourist, who raised his hands.

I backed away, until I bumped up against the keys of a piano. They made no sound. The entire instrument was made of cardboard.

"Anything can be haunted if you wish it to be," said one of the preservationists suddenly, like a released spring. "Ghosts are tumors of the imagination. Instead of renovating old hospitals, abandoned factories, you permit them to decay. You celebrate stagnant, broken forms and shirk the responsibility to bring them back to life." The preservationist's tall frame rattled.

"You spend obscene amounts of money on plasma

detectors and high-definition microphones, nonsense equipment, just because you don't know how to clean debris from a room to imagine new possibilities. Instead you take pictures of lost towns where life has passed through them like a sieve. Instead of innovation you take an *opera house* like *this* and turn it into a *site* for your irreverence."

The jolly tourist, stunned, tried to express that he didn't feel this way, but the preservationists were somewhere else, haunted by the difficult task of keeping alive someone who was of no consequence to neighboring towns who viewed them as ghosts, their treasure at stake on a larger stage, unrelated to us or our foolish mention of hauntings.

We were shepherded back into the sun. The preservationists, distressed, cut the tour short. Even their blue dresses now looked wrinkly and pale. We thanked them and they went back to their rooms. We stood in the sand. The jolly tourist pulled his face with his hands and made a horrified facial expression, similar to the preservationists'. He laughed.

He gestured to me with a skinny pale finger. "And you?" he said. "Are you a performer or something?" He wiggled his eyebrows toward the opera house.

"I teach. Film studies, but I've been on leave," I said.

He asked if I had seen Zabriskie Point. I nodded eagerly, relaying to him the experience I had driving through there to get to Badwater, when I prayed and the bottom of the world seemed to have fallen off, and I knew that God himself had caught me. Though I didn't fully understand it yet—I continued breathlessly—I felt committed to pursuing a life formed by faith. My hands began to quiver slightly. The jolly tourist looked at me with solid eyes and a moment passed before I realized he had meant *Zabriskie Point*, the Antonioni film.

"Oh, yes, gosh, I've seen it," I explained quickly, and was surprised that I hadn't remembered it when I was there.

The jolly tourist laughed, undeterred. His hair was like fire, and it swept and flickered as he extended his arm toward the landscape all around. I was relieved. My pursuits had always revolved around representations of life instead of life itself. Like medieval scribes, who traced the ornamented shapes of words without knowing what they meant or how to read them. It seemed to be a good sign that I saw a place for what it was.

The jolly tourist was on his way to the singing sands of Eureka Dunes, where the sand slides at a certain angle and the friction creates a sound of a low note on a pipe organ. Nature's beautiful music, he said, using finger quotes. He asked if I would like to come along, and for a moment I wished to. I could imagine the brief thrill of adventuring with him, or the way his arms would feel wrapped around me, but I declined, and, perhaps inspired by the preservationist's haunting tirade, I possessed a brighter eagerness to return home.

He placed his hand on my shoulder, stepping closer so that we fully faced each other. Something stirred and flew away. He moved back, got into his car, rolled down his window. We smiled for a long time before he drove away, leaving a sweet feeling, sweet like the smell of ambergris.

Every ten years, a superbloom came to Death Valley. The dried ground brought forth every kind of flower—

> desert golds, stars, and trumpets
> Eureka Dunes evening primrose
> grape soda lupine
> wavyleaf desert paintbrush
> and mariposa lilies . . .

The superbloom surprised me when I packed the white convertible to leave. The flowers were everywhere, like the tamarisk trees against the adobe. A testament to how everything operated this way. Nothing fretted by death, but instead prospering through spans and ends. Even Amargosa, a name meaning "bitter," pushed forth swathes of petals.

I was always under the impression that the parable of the mustard seed was a trick about proportion—that something as small as a seed produced something large like faith, and that the smallness and largeness were defined by the sizes at the beginning and end stages of a mustard plant. What I hadn't understood was that mustard is a weed, one that grows fast. This mustard seed is interested in movement, and a single seed grows up to multiply across vast distances, ungovernable and wild like language. The scope changes, then, from a seed that flourishes into one tall individual presence, to many seeds that sweep across the surface of the earth, garden by garden, until the very last plot.

When Marta died, her ashes were strewn about Death Valley Junction with wildflower seed, and I liked to imagine that it included night-blooming cereus, which blooms once a year for a single night. It blooms five feet across, white like a moon, the brightest thing in the time of shadows, only to fold itself up at the first beam of day. A sliver of proof that from oblivion can come intentional precision. John Cage, in a completely soundproof room, listened hard and close to hear two tones emerge, one high and one low—one of his nervous system and the other of his blood circulation. Mendelssohn sat in a cave and heard the opening of The Hebrides. Marta looked through a small hole in the wall and saw an opera house. I thought I had nothing, but after long enough something emerged from bitter water—a mysterious thing that precedes itself, and continues past itself, a master of ceremonies who stands outside the beginning and end.

Before driving through the Funeral Mountains to the airport, I collected armfuls and armfuls of those superbloom flowers from the fields of sand, and laid them onto the dining room table and chairs for the preservationists in thanks.

On the airplane, I flipped through a local newspaper that I snagged from the lobby of the Amargosa Hotel. There were library events and death notices, an article on how to protect the rare species of guppy found in puddles in the valley, and a column on car repair.

One picture in the newspaper caught my attention: an old, chuffed man in an alpine hat standing in front of a Tudor cottage. It appeared that the man and his house were from the past, except that the cottage was set against the sprawling desert, and a billboard loomed in the background advertising a casino lunch buffet.

What followed the photograph was somewhat of a book review. The newspaper writer described an experience of recalling an absorbing and fashionable novel from his youth, written by the man with an alpine hat in the photograph. The novel, the newspaper writer described, was so popular that it was often passed between classes, read in the fields, carried around even when finished. All the kids in his school read this tale, which took place in the Subcarpathian mountains of old Ruthenia, of a young shepherd who saved the village from a life-sucking ruler with "only his integrity." This obscure region—nestled between former Czechoslovakia and Hungary—was described with such vibrance and intimacy that the children of the newspaper writer's school longed to visit it, the way children wish to visit *the sea* or *the Wild West*, with its sweet soul pain and blue forests, vineyards along the rivers of the mountains, filled with painters and unlikely heroes.

This article, however, was not about that novel. This article went on to describe a discovery that neither the author nor any of his kin had ever been out of America, but that he had written the book from jail while serving an arson sentence. How—wondered this tedious, moss-grown book critic—could he have imagined such specificity from a cold dark cell? Faced with minor resentments and a dividing reception from the public about the novel's success, the man in the alpine hat resorted to setting his next books in America, a place he was closely familiar with, and the newspaper writer, who read those novels too, thought they were absolutely mediocre.

What the article settled on was that sometimes people feel most intensely what they cannot see, and that this feeling is a gift. That this man, who grew up in an empty Texan town and never left it, had some sort of access to a place in the past through an amplification of the heart, in a way that could never have existed with the places he was blinded to by familiarity. Not dissimilar to the presence of God in someone's life, ventured the newspaper writer, which was also a phenomenon that involved a magnifying and stirring and knocking, often against the heart-bearer's will.

The newspaper writer found that the author, with the intention of writing the book he had always wanted (or thought he had wanted), eventually *did* visit a mountain village in Europe, later in life. During his time there, he became a drunk and a melancholic, befriended a man whose image was illegally used on the health warnings of cigarette packs, entered a despaired love affair with a postal clerk, ceased writing, then returned home with a scar above his jaw. In the time that followed, his father wrote him many letters, urging him that the beauty and creativity he longed for couldn't be found from some village, postal clerk, or material circumstance.

The article ended with an announcement that the author's next and final novel, about self-healing, would be published later in the winter, and that the inner child of the newspaper writer was excited for what it would yield.

I returned to the photograph of the man in his alpine hat. He settled for the world until wind brought him back up to the heavens. I folded the newspaper and put it into the seat pocket in front of me.

Flight attendants came to check on me. I looked out the window, imagining mustard seeds spreading across the ground below at the speed of airplane travel. I was thirsty and someone brought me water. I drank it.

4

My mother tends a small garden, but considers it a gift. "How can I expect anything more if I can't care for what I have?" she says, removing pale grubs from the soil. She places them writhing on a black stone in the sun for birds to find. She collects the harvest from tomato plants, corn, beets, and places the excess on the neighbors' steps.

I help her weed and dig. She goes inside to wash her hands and make some tea. I hear her from the open door. Some pink laughter.

Instead of shadow mapping, she's begun mapping the sun. Her eyes are going, she says, and she has a better time tracking light. She tells me about Carl Linnaeus, an eighteenth-century plant taxonomist, who made a "botanical clock," an entire garden made up of groupings of plants that bloom when the sun directly falls on them. At 7:00 a.m. the petals of the St. Bernard's lily open, and a sweet smell fills the garden. Promptly at 8:00 a.m. they close. The phlox plant opens at 9:00 a.m. and it smells like musk. Day after day the plants take their turns to perform. I wonder how difficult it would be to attempt a flower clock in my own empty backyard.

In the evening she boils fruit for preserves while I read aloud. I describe the jolly tourist and she says that a boisterous friend would suit me.

A week later I ask someone from my new job if he'd like to go on a walk. I send my mother close-ups of things we find. She finds things for me as well. Collecting and offering, finding grubs for the black stone.

Joy completed and doubly felt. The world seen twice as well, like a windowpane made from a prescription lens. Some nights I feel the renounced dark, sticky melancholy lap back, and I strike gray with panic. I'm attempting to catch the dust as it falls. We pray for that too, along with each day's mercy and health, our acquaintances. Like a barn swallow's forked tail. Time spent with one another, doubly spent with God.

I receive an email from the preservationists, detailing a recent attempt to replace the roof of the opera house, and announcing that tours have started up again. Plumbing is next, then new furniture, but the worry remains. Recently a bandit roamed the hotel room windows, and a painting went missing from the lobby.

During one of my weekly visits, I fix a light in my mother's basement. The walls are stained and musty, boxes of papers line the floor. I sort through one while I hear my mother walk upstairs, go outside, then inside.

She calls for me, forgetting where I went. I sing out, I'm here.

Acknowledgments

Special thanks to Jordan Castro, Yuka Igarashi, and Alexander Reubert. Cynthia Talmadge, who painted this cover with sand. Maud Casey, Howard Norman, Christian Wiman, Scott McClanahan, Milo Conroy, Megan Boyle, Juliet Escoria, Valeria Lamarra, Marika Proctor, Beata and Jozef Polek, Constance L. Casey and Harold E. Varmus, and the Rona Jaffe Foundation. Fred Conboy for opening up the doors of the Amargosa Opera House.

My mother for her faith, and God who supplies the strength to continue.

Quotations and biographical details come from *To Dance on Sands* by Marta Becket, and *Amargosa*, a documentary by Todd Robinson.